THE KING OF KUMARI KANDAM

Adapted by I. Trimble
Illustrated by Scott Jeralds

A STEPPING STONE BOOK™

Random House 🏠 New York

Visit us on the Web!
www.randomhouse.com/kids

Educators and librarians, for a variety of teaching tools, visit us at
www.randomhouse.com/teachers

Library of Congress Cataloging-in-Publication Data
Trimble, Irene.
The king of Kumari Kandam / adapted by I. Trimble ; illustrated by Scott Jeralds. — 1st ed.
p. cm.

ISBN 978-0-375-86429-2 (trade) — 978-0-375-96429-9 (library binding)
I. Jeralds, Scott. II. Secret Saturdays (Television program). III. Title.
PZ7.T735185Kin 2009
[Fic]—dc22
2009005109
www.randomhouse.com/kids
Printed in the United States of America
10 9 8 7 6 5 4 3 2 1

Chapter 1

Night fell as the Saturday family's airship hovered over the forests of Zanzibar. The adventurous Saturdays were in search of yet another elusive cryptid on the tiny African island. This time, they were after the Devil's Cave Bird. The purple, batlike Devil's Cave Bird would make an interesting addition to the list of cryptids they'd already discovered.

Cryptids were rare creatures that most people thought were just the stuff of myths and legends. But like most myths and legends, sometimes there was a little bit of truth behind them. The Saturdays' job was to seek out cryptids and, if they proved to be real, to collect as much information about them as possible.

Doc Saturday, a world-famous scientist and supergenius, was in the airship's minigym. He and his wife, Drew, were warming up with a series of kicks and punches.

Like most moms, Drew wanted to be completely prepared if her family had to face danger. And legend had it that the Devil's Cave Bird could be savage if disturbed.

Drew pushed up to a handstand and took a few upside-down kicks at Doc. He calmly blocked them. Doc told her he preferred to use the element of surprise rather than brute force.

As Doc and Drew Saturday continued to spar, their eleven-year-old son, Zak Saturday, quietly crept through the minigym door. It was really late—two hours past his bedtime. No one would expect him to be up now.

Zak silently dove, rolled, and flipped from shadow to shadow until he had crossed the gym. He was trying to get to the airship's helm without being noticed—and he was almost there.

"Still with me, Komodo?" he whispered, looking around for his pet Komodo dragon.

Komodo was a cryptid that Zak had talked his parents into keeping as a family pet. Komodo was the size of a large dog and just as loyal. And like many reptiles, he could instantly camouflage himself to become almost invisible in any environment.

Komodo became visible, and Zak patted the green dragon's head. The young Saturday had a special bond with cryptids. He could calm them—and sometimes control them—with his mind, as long as they weren't one of the more

powerful or vicious varieties.

"Good boy. Get ready. Now!" Zak said as he and Komodo darted into the helm of the ship. Zak rushed to the largest monitor in the room and began to adjust the controls.

Behind him, two red eyes blinked open and gleamed in the darkness. A menacing shape loomed over Zak in the light of the glowing screen. Zak did not see it sneaking up behind him!

"Hey, Fiskerton," Zak said without taking his eyes off the monitor. "Got any popcorn?"

The shape slipped down onto the couch next to Zak—and offered the boy some popcorn from the bucket he was holding in his furry hand. Fiskerton was another cryptid. But he wasn't a pet. Fiskerton was more like Zak's half-cat, half-gorilla brother. And he stood about seven feet tall and was covered in grayish green and brown fur.

And he really loved snack food.

Zak took a handful of popcorn from the bucket, and he and Fiskerton settled onto the couch just as an image appeared on the monitor. It showed the creepy interior of a mummy's tomb. The title of Zak's favorite TV show, *V. V. Argost's Weirdworld,* suddenly flashed on the screen.

Zak loved *Weirdworld.* Argost featured different writhing, howling cryptids week after week. Most viewers thought they were fakes, just TV fun. But Zak knew better—his life involved cryptids on a daily basis.

Argost also happened to be his father's archenemy. So technically, Zak was not allowed to watch the show—*ever*. But hey, it was good television.

"Aw, yeah, here we go!" Zak said as Argost's evil laugh filled the room.

Argost's assistant, Munya, appeared and slowly opened an elaborately carved sarcophagus. Argost was inside, wrapped in a straightjacket, laughing like a madman.

Zak watched as Munya took a long knife and split the restraints open, setting his master free. Argost stepped out with the flourish of an expert showman. He looked into the camera and said, "Greetings and *bienvenue*. I, the incomparable V. V. Argost, welcome you to my humble mansion of the macabre. You know how we love our visitors here at *Weirdworld*."

Argost plucked a small lizard from the wall and popped it into his mouth.

From the corner of the room, a winged blue pterosaur cringed. It was Zon, Zak's other cryptid friend.

"Relax," Zak told the flying reptile, wanting to keep her quiet during the show. "It's a fake.

It's made out of that gummy stuff."

Zon grumbled and went back to eating a fish.

Munya pulled down a map as Argost crooned, "Tonight we are searching for the lost city of Kumari Kandam." A model of the island kingdom sat on a table. Argost waved his hand over the replica, and it was suddenly hit with every disaster known to man.

Zak watched the little city as it was rocked by earthquakes, bombarded with tidal waves, and swallowed into the sea. In a blinding flash, it was gone!

"Sweet," Zak said as he stuffed another handful of popcorn into his mouth.

"Sadly, this jewel was taken before her time," Argost said, motioning to the ripple on the smoking water. "Ripped from the mainland, she was cast down like that mighty Atlantis to the black, bottomless sea, where the world foolishly believed she would remain for all eternity!"

Argost took a moment to laugh wildly.

"But," Argost said, returning to his grim story, "you and I know better, don't we, children? Having been entombed more than once myself, I can tell you this from experience: no matter how many times you shove them beneath the surface, some things simply refuse to stay buried."

Zak and other viewers around the world didn't know it, but Argost was talking about real events. At that very moment, a small freighter in the Indian Ocean was being brutally attacked. Laser fire was hailing down on the freighter's crewmen. The city of Kumari Kandam had returned!

Chapter 2

Bright and early the following morning, the Saturdays were stealthily approaching a large nest on the island of Zanzibar.

"Oh-six-thirty Zulu time. Negative sighting of Devil's Cave Bird at nesting tree," Doc whispered into the electronic Cryptopedia on his wrist. Doc had invented the Cryptopedia. He called it a CP for short. It held a database of known cryptids.

As the Saturdays hid in the tall grass, Zak slowly blinked and yawned. He was still tired from his secret TV viewing.

"Late night, sweetheart?" his mom asked.

"Uh, no," Zak replied. He didn't want her to suspect that he had been watching V. V. Argost's show. Zak's mom gave him a look that said she was suspicious anyway. And to make matters worse, Fiskerton and Komodo had dark circles under their eyes, too.

"Let's keep it together," Doc Saturday said. "We don't want anyone getting hurt, including the Devil's Cave Bird. For now, we only want to confirm it exists."

Drew pointed out the eggs in the nest. She said if the eggs belonged to the Devil's Cave Bird, the creature would reveal itself sooner or later.

When Komodo heard the word "eggs," his drowsy eyes snapped open. He licked his lips and made a mad dash for the nest.

"Bad Komodo dragon!" Zak scolded.

Fiskerton broke from his hiding place in the grass and raced ahead of Komodo. Fiskerton was tall enough to snatch the eggs out of the nest before Komodo could climb up and eat them.

"Bad dog," Fiskerton growled as Komodo tried to climb his leg to get to the eggs.

Exasperated, Doc threw up his hands. "So much for stealth," he grumbled. He charged up his stun weapon in case the Devil's Cave Bird came to check on her nest.

"Hey! You can't just zap Komodo!" Zak yelled.

"It's not a zap," Doc said as he calmly checked the Cortex Disrupter's display panel. "It's a harmless scrambling of the intercranial neuron flow!"

A shriek from the sky suddenly ended the conversation. Fiskerton looked up and cringed. The Devil's Cave Bird had returned to her nest, and he was still holding her eggs!

The leathery-winged Devil's Cave Bird dove

at Fiskerton with her long talons extended. He tossed the eggs into the air and ran for cover.

The creature caught her eggs in midair and flew off, barely clearing Zak's head.

"Sooo . . . ," Zak said as he smoothed the part in his hair made by the Devil's Cave Bird, "I'm pretty sure it exists."

As the Saturdays made their way back to the airship, Zak pondered aloud, "You know what would have made that go better?"

"If we'd gotten a dog for a pet?" Drew replied sarcastically.

Komodo gave her a hiss.

"No," Zak said, "I think I should have my own Cortex Disrupter."

Drew Saturday yelled, *"What?"*

"Whoa, Mom! It's not a big deal. We have plenty of them."

"I think your mother is asking why you think you should have one," Doc said calmly.

"Well, I'm part of the team, right?" Zak asked. But *that* didn't seem to be enough to convince his mother, either.

"That cryptid came right at me," Zak said, trying a different argument. "Isn't this a safety issue?"

Doc looked at the Hand of Tsul'Kalu hanging on Zak's belt. It could help Zak stop a cryptid better than any Cortex Disrupter—once he'd really mastered it.

"You feel unsafe while packing a multi-function adaptive weapon that focuses your cryptid-influencing powers?" his father asked.

Zak sighed. "No, the Claw's great," he replied, giving in. "But we're still figuring my powers out.

I need something with some kick."

His parents looked at him, still skeptical. "Hey, I'm eleven years old now," Zak argued. "I think you can trust me."

"Really?" his dad asked. "This from a boy who snuck past his parents to watch Argost's show last night?"

Zak cringed. *How did his father always know?* Doc rubbed his temples. The whole discussion was giving him a headache.

"Well, there's no way my baby is getting a Cortex Disrupter," Drew said.

"I'm just wondering if it would be a good lesson in responsibility," Doc replied.

Suddenly, Zon started screeching. She was still aboard their airship.

Doc pulled out his machete and began slashing through the tall grass. When the Saturdays arrived at the airship, Zon was still screeching.

A red light was flashing over one of the video monitors. Doc activated the telecommunications console.

Dr. Odele, a secret scientist and a good friend of Doc's, appeared on the monitor. His clothes were torn and his face was covered in soot. The sounds of a battle were raging behind him.

"Odele, where are you?" Doc asked in shock.

"An atoll in the Indian Ocean," Odele gasped. "My team of researchers and I have been attacked."

"Who attacked?" Drew asked.

"It appears to be Kumari Kandam!" Odele answered.

Odele turned his camera toward the beach. A huge floating city was firing laser blasts at the tiny atoll. Then suddenly the screen went blank!

Drew jumped into the pilot's seat. She looked

over her shoulder at Zak and Fiskerton. "Buckle up," she told them. "We're leaving now."

As the airship zoomed toward the Indian Ocean, Doc explained to Zak that Kumari Kandam was an ancient city that could supposedly travel underwater. No one knew how such a feat could have been accomplished.

"Kumari legend says the city moves by the magic of their gods," Drew added. She tended to believe in more mystical explanations for things.

"Clearly," Doc said, not believing such supernatural poppycock, "the Kumari must have tapped a primitive but effective power source to fuel their engines."

Drew smiled. "Like the magic of their gods."

Doc gritted his teeth. "Or electrokinetic energy."

"Sounds pretty dangerous," Zak said, nodding.

He had his mind on only one thing. "Just to be safe, I should probably have a Cortex Disrupter."

"No!" his parents said in unison.

Chapter 3

It wasn't long before the airship was flying over the Indian Ocean. The Saturdays could see heavy laser fire pummeling a small atoll in the distance.

Dr. Odele was on the beach, waving his arms. "We surrender!" he shouted toward Kumari Kandam. The ancient city was floating just offshore.

Meanwhile, a Kumari captain strutted along the observation deck. He was quite satisfied with the victory.

"A successful artillery exercise," the captain

said smugly to an admiral. "Does the king have any further orders?"

A figure hidden in the shadows gave the admiral a nod.

"Sink the island," the admiral told the captain.

The captain was about to give the signal to fire when the Saturdays' airship swooped down between the city and the atoll.

Drew jumped out of the hovering airship. She began broadcasting from her headset. "Citizens of Kumari Kandam, I humbly offer to negotiate peace with your people."

A wicked voice was broadcast back: "Tempting, my dear."

From the airship, Doc and Zak watched the shadowy figure walk into the palace courtyard. The man was wearing a silvery cape made from the skin of a megatooth shark. There was only one cape like it in the world—and it belonged to V. V. Argost!

"Thank you for your generous offer," the evil madman said with a sneer, "but His Royal Highness, *me*, respectfully declines. Sorry."

The Kumari rotated their cannons and fired harpoon cables at the airship. One cable wrapped around Drew's leg and began to reel her in.

"Mom!" Zak yelled. He and his father jumped to her aid.

Drew unsheathed the Tibetan Fire Sword from the scabbard on her back. The sword burst into flames when it was exposed to the sunlight. With a swipe of the fiery blade, she cut herself free and fell to the ground.

Zak watched as a wave of Kumari soldiers charged at them. He helped his mother to her feet. More soldiers were using the harpoon lines to slide down the palace walls.

Zak climbed onto Fiskerton's shoulders. Together they battled the Kumari soldiers zipping down the lines.

"If you were having second thoughts about not giving me a Cortex Disrupter," Zak yelled to his dad, "now would be the time for one!"

But Doc was too busy to disagree or to hand out Cortex Disrupters. The fight was on! Doc took on soldier after soldier in hand-to-hand combat. He was a master of fourteen different martial arts—and he was using every move he knew to keep the soldiers at bay.

Meanwhile, Drew swung her blazing sword, scattering soldiers in every direction. Fiskerton struck the soldiers with his huge hands and feet. Zak batted at them with the Claw. Komodo used his camouflaging powers to appear and disappear, biting soldiers as he went. Zon struck from above, scratching with her claws. But in the end, the Saturdays were outnumbered. Doc and Drew were mobbed.

Before the soldiers could get Zak and

Fiskerton, Drew yelled, "Get to the airship and get out of here!"

Using all her strength, Drew pulled her arm free and threw her sword into the air. The whirling blade sliced through the cables that held the airship.

Fiskerton tucked Zak under his arm like a football and ran.

"Let me go!" Zak yelled, still wanting to fight. He didn't want to leave his parents behind.

Fiskerton leapt into the airship and randomly hit every control button on the instrument panel until the airship started to rise.

"Noooooo!" Zak yelled, unable to do anything but watch.

Below, in the palace courtyard, Argost looked up at the departing airship. Doc and Drew were tied and kneeling at his feet.

"Ahh, it's good to be king," Argost declared with a smile.

Chapter 4

Inside the cold, dark Kumari prison, Doc and Drew were tossed into a dank, seaweed-covered cell.

"Careful with the female," Argost said to the guards with a smile. "She's quite feisty."

Drew lunged for Argost. The guards knocked her back with their electrified spears. Argost laughed when the cell door slammed shut.

Doc began to examine the walls of the cell—they needed to find a way to escape. But in the back of his mind, he was thinking about the day's events. They *had* to have something to do with Argost's ongoing plan to find the third piece of the mysterious Kur Stone. With the stone, he could master an ancient Sumerian cryptid named Kur that was powerful enough to take over the world.

Argost possessed two parts of the stone already. The Saturdays had the third and last piece safely hidden away.

"Nothing on our stone piece suggests that Kumari Kandam is part of the puzzle to finding Kur," Doc said, thinking aloud. "But if Argost has taken over the city, then logically, there must be something on one of the pieces Argost has that's led him here."

"Doc!" Drew said with her hands on her hips. "How can you be so logical right now?"

Doc nodded—getting out of the cell had to come first.

He pulled a strand of seaweed off the wall
and looked at it carefully.

High above the prison in the airship, Zak was
slipping into a glider harness attached to Zon. He
and Zon left the airship and silently glided to a
dock at the edge of the city below.

Fiskerton suddenly leapt out of the airship
and into the water with Komodo in his arms—
SPLASH!

"So much for stealth," Zak grumbled. Zon
shook the water from her wings, drenching Zak.
Then she took off back to the airship.

Zak, Fiskerton, and Komodo quietly crept
toward the city. As they passed a dark alley, a
hand reached out and grabbed Zak's arm. In an
instant, Fiskerton pounced on the attacker. The

big gorilla-cat held him to the ground as Komodo poked at him with his snout.

Zak looked at his attacker's face. He was just a little kid.

"You have got to be about the weakest spy I have ever seen," Zak said.

"Unhand me!" the boy said arrogantly. "I am not a spy. I am Ulraj, the king of Kumari Kandam!"

Zak wasn't buying it.

"You don't believe me?" Ulraj asked. He pulled out a gold medallion and showed it to Zak. "Then argue with this!"

Zak looked at it. The medallion was covered with bright stones and writing in an unknown language. Zak rolled his eyes.

"Wow, Fisk. I don't know how we're going to argue with a necklace," Zak teased, trying not to laugh. "Hey, remember that glitter pen I had that

made me emperor of Venus?"

Fiskerton chuckled heartily.

Ulraj said, "I can help you find your parents."

Zak stopped laughing. Fiskerton gave him a look that said *It's worth a try*. Zak helped the kid to his feet.

Zak, Fiskerton, and Komodo followed Ulraj to a rooftop overlooking the palace. They could see Argost walking through the large palace doors with Munya.

"They arrived two weeks ago," Ulraj said sadly. He told them how it had all begun.

Kumari Kandam had been encased in a watertight bubble beneath the sea, just as it had been for centuries, before Argost and Munya arrived.

"Argost told my father, the king, that he'd come to warn us," Ulraj explained. "He said the surface men had found our city once again and were preparing to destroy us."

As if on cue, a huge explosion had rocked the city. They were attacked by a fleet of minisubs. Argost had directed the Kumari soldiers in a counterattack. His help had enabled them to destroy the minisubs. Argost was made a hero. Ulraj and his father were the only ones who suspected that Argost had really sent the attackers. It had all been a trick to put himself in power.

"But my father was wounded terribly during the fighting," Ulraj told Zak. "He placed this necklace around my neck and said with his last breath, 'Run while you still can.' That's when Argost took control and made himself king. Within days, he was preparing the city for war."

Zak felt sorry for the prince. "I knew Argost was bad," he said, shaking his head. "But that's just sick." Fiskerton grumbled in agreement.

Ulraj nodded. He explained to Zak that he would have confronted Argost himself, but he had no plan, no army, and no weapons.

Zak lit up when he heard the word "weapons," just like Komodo did whenever he heard the word "egg."

"We may not have a plan, or an army," Zak said, thinking about all the Cortex Disrupters stored in the airship. "But I wouldn't exactly say we have no weapons."

Chapter 5

Inside the prison, Doc and Drew were busy hatching a plan for their escape. "You realize if I have calculated incorrectly, this will be extremely painful," Doc said as they wrapped wet seaweed around a metal bar on the cell door.

"Good thing you're a supergenius," Drew teased. She gave her husband a kiss on the forehead.

Just then, a Kumari guard passed the cell.

"Help! Please!" Drew shouted, putting the plan

into action. "My husband is very sick! He needs medical help immediately!"

The guard looked into the cell. Doc was doubled over in pain. The guard smirked. "Did you think we wouldn't have that trick down here, too?"

He was about to walk away when Drew yelled, "No, I was just thinking you were as stupid as you smell!"

The guard growled and hurled himself at the cell door in a fury. That was Doc's signal to attach the strand of seaweed to his CP and let it rip. The guard screamed as a jolt of electricity coursed through the metal door.

Drew tore the strand of seaweed with her foot to break the current. The guard fell to the floor in a twitching heap. "Bet you don't have *that* trick down here," she said as she reached through the bars and took his keys.

As Doc and Drew prepared to make their way out of prison, Zak was high above, plotting his way in.

Zak, Ulraj, Komodo, and Fiskerton stood in front of the airship's high-tech weapons vault. The heavy door was firmly locked.

Zak gave Fiskerton a nod. It was time for some muscle. "Do your thing, Fisk," Zak said, waiting for the superstrong gorilla-cat to punch in the vault door.

But Fiskerton wouldn't budge.

"I know what Mom and Dad said," Zak pleaded, "but this is an emergency! It's not like we're going on a rampage."

Ulraj proclaimed, "As king of Kumari Kandam, I order you to—"

But Zak held up his hand before the impatient

prince could finish. "Not helping," Zak said.

Zak told Fiskerton they were just going to zap Argost, then force him to release Doc and Drew and give back Ulraj's kingdom. Just like that. Done. Weapons back in the box. "How could Mom and Dad argue with that?" Zak reasoned.

Fiskerton still wasn't sure, but he growled, "What the heck." POW! He punched the vault door so hard it flew open, revealing several glowing Cortex Disrupters.

"Ho, yeah!" Zak said, taking in the sight. Then he turned to Ulraj. "Now, where do we find that phony king?"

Chapter 6

In the palace courtyard of Kumari Kandam, a large crowd was gathering to hear King Argost speak. Doc and Drew Saturday moved secretly among the Kumari. The two adventurers were wearing the uniforms of their Kumari prison guards. Their disguises seemed to be working.

Soon they saw Argost and Munya come out onto the palace steps.

"He's right there!" Drew whispered. "Let's just take him!"

"Not yet," Doc said cautiously. "We need to

know what's going on here."

Argost raised his arms and the crowd went silent. "Brothers and sisters of Kumari Kandam," Argost said, shaking his head, "I have troubling news. The surface man and woman escaped during the night."

The crowd gasped. They began to chant, "Destroy the surface men! Destroy the surface men!" Doc and Drew nervously pulled their hooded robes around their faces a bit tighter as the crowd got more agitated.

On a rooftop above, Zak and Komodo watched the scene. Komodo had the grappling cable from the Claw attached to his back.

Zak's weapon had lots of uses. It was sometimes a defensive staff for blocking punches and kicks or a pole for vaulting out of tight situations. The Hand of Tsul'Kalu had an expandable cable attached to it so that Zak could use it as a grappling hook. The device also helped him focus his cryptid-influencing powers. But he was still working on that.

"We're in position," Zak said into his headset. "Is Zon ready to get us out after we grab Argost?"

Ulraj and Fiskerton were in the airship.

"Yes," Ulraj answered. "Zon is ready."

Fiskerton pulled on a pair of aviator sunglasses and reached for the controls. Ulraj frowned. He slapped Fiskerton's hand away. "Zak says I am not to let you touch the buttons!" The big gorilla-cat slumped and grumbled.

Below, Argost was still stirring up the crowd. "These surface men have been inside our city. They know our weaknesses," he said to the angry Kumari. "They struck us once. They will strike us again unless we act first!"

The crowd began yelling for war.

"We have to stop this!" Drew said to Doc. She started to make her move on Argost.

"Ready?" Zak asked Komodo as they prepared to leap into action at the same moment.

Komodo backed up a few steps, and Zak gave him the go-ahead. Komodo jumped off the roof with the Claw's cable trailing behind him. When he reached the opposite wall, the cable snapped tight.

Zak slid down the cable, landing only a few feet from Argost.

Argost gasped.

Zak looked him straight in the eye and squeezed the trigger of the Cortex Disrupter.

But at that same instant, Drew reached the top of the steps. She lunged for Argost—

accidentally coming between Argost and the Disrupter's beam. ZAP! The blast hit her full-force.

Zak dropped the Cortex Disrupter in shock as he watched his mother tumble down the steps.

"Mom!" Zak shouted.

Argost lost no time taking control. "They attack already!" he yelled to the crowd. "Strike now!"

Munya and the Kumari admiral lunged for Zak. But Zak's instinct to save his mother took over. He somersaulted down the steps to where Drew was lying.

Doc broke through the crowd. He picked Drew up in his arms.

"I'm so sorry," Zak whispered.

Doc knew he had to get Drew back to the airship to save her. They were going to have to fight their way there.

Doc began to push against the angry throng of Kumari. Just then, Komodo leapt from the wall and began clearing a path with vicious bites. Zak dropped to one knee and made leg sweeps to take out the guards from below. Komodo tossed Kumaris this way and that.

The three fought their way to the edge of the city. They dove into the water and swam toward the airship.

Back at the palace, Argost used what had happened to his full advantage. He cried out, "Great Kumari, let us strike a blow the surface men will never forget! We move for land—and war!"

Argost smiled wickedly as the Kumari raised their weapons and cheered.

Chapter 7

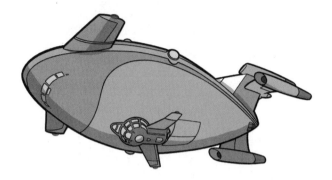

The Saturdays finally surfaced near the hovering airship. Doc was swimming with Drew in his arms.

"Is she okay?" Zak asked, terrified that she wasn't.

"She's alive," Doc replied gruffly. He was upset with his son. "What were you thinking, Zak?"

"I was trying to rescue you," Zak replied. "I just wanted to get you guys back."

"We need to get your mother to the medical equipment on the airship," Doc said gently. "Do

you have any way of reaching it?"

Zak nodded in the direction of the airship. It suddenly dropped out of the sky and came in close for a rescue.

As the hatch door popped open, Fiskerton leaned out, extending his hand to help. He was smiling and wearing his aviator sunglasses.

"I let him touch the buttons," Ulraj said.

Once they were aboard, Doc quickly examined Drew in the ship's medical unit. "She's going to be okay," he told Zak.

Zak let out a huge sigh of relief.

"I am very glad to hear that," Ulraj said.

Doc looked at the boy. "Thank you," he said. "Who are you?"

"I am Ulraj, king of Kumari Kandam."

Doc was confused for a moment.

"Don't try arguing," Zak told Doc. "He's got the jewelry to prove it."

At that moment, a groaning roar came from outside the ship. They all rushed to the helm. The city of Kumari Kandam was uncoiling like a giant snake!

"What's happening?" Zak asked.

Ulraj hung his head. "It's war. Kumari Kandam is moving."

"Moving how?" Doc asked.

The head of a huge sea serpent rose from the water. Doc realized that this was the unknown source of Kumari Kandam's power. The entire city had been built on the leviathan's back.

"Whoa!" Zak exclaimed.

Doc thought for a moment. He looked at Ulraj and said, "Argost doesn't care about ruling Kumari Kandam at all. He wants its king . . . or something the king can give him."

"Where did the medallion come from originally?" Doc asked.

When Ulraj told him it was an ancient gift from the Sumerian dynasty, Doc smiled. He knew what Argost was up to now. The Sumerian writings on the medallion would help Argost locate Kur. The people of Kumari Kandam had simply been a means to that end.

"Your Highness," Doc told Ulraj, "you have a powerful and dangerous artifact here."

Doc came up with a plan. He, Ulraj, and Fiskerton would go down to Kumari Kandam. "Zak, that leaves you to stop the sea serpent from reaching land."

Zak was stunned. "You want me to take on a gigantic sea serpent by myself? That thing might be a little out of the league of my cryptid powers!"

Doc knew that his son's powers were still a bit shaky. He opened the weapons vault and took out a Cortex Disrupter.

"And that's why you're going to need one of these," Doc said. Taking a look at the sea serpent out the window, he added, "Probably several bundled together."

Doc tried to hand his son the weapon, but Zak didn't want anything to do with it. "Whoa! Dad! I know you were the one who wanted me to have a Disrupter in the first place, but no! No way!"

"What I wanted was a way to teach you responsibility," Doc said. "You made a terrible choice, but now the responsible thing to do is to try to make it right."

Zak nodded.

"Your mother was hurt trying to stop a war," Doc said. "It's up to us to finish it!"

Chapter 8

Argost sat on his throne in the Kumari palace. He was pleased to hear the admiral report that their forces had reach the mainland.

"Splendid!" Argost told him. "Order your men to strike immediately."

The large palace doors suddenly creaked open. Everyone was shocked to see Ulraj standing alone in the doorway.

"I wish to speak to Argost and his servant," Ulraj announced.

Argost beamed. "Certainly, Your Majesty!"

"Alone!" Ulraj demanded.

"Even better," Argost said with evil delight.

After the admiral and the palace guards had left, Ulraj told Argost, "I know why you've come here. And soon all my people will know."

Argost snickered at the boy and grinned at Munya. "Oh, I do find that hard to believe."

"And why is that?" Ulraj asked.

"Because in ten seconds, you're going to be much too terrified to say anything ever again."

Argost laughed and gave Munya a nod. The lumbering servant activated his DNA injector.

Ulraj was indeed terrified to see Munya sprout the fangs and legs of an arachnid. Munya became half spider, half man.

"Munya," Argost said confidently, "if you would do the honors."

Munya scrambled on his huge spider legs

toward Ulraj. His long arms reached for Ulraj's neck. Cringing in horror, Ulraj felt the hairy spider legs on his skin as Munya ripped his shirt open.

"What!" Argost exclaimed. Ulraj's amulet was not there!

Doc Saturday's voice suddenly echoed through the room. "You didn't think I'd hand you another clue to finding Kur?" he said, taunting his archenemy.

Argost was furious! He and Munya looked up. Doc was hanging on to Fiskerton's back as the big cryptid climbed down a stone column to the palace floor.

"Now," Doc said, jumping down to face Argost, "I believe you're sitting on this young man's throne."

"Munya!" Argost yelled in a fury.

The spiderlike henchman charged at Doc and Fiskerton, knocking them to the ground.

Outside the palace, the fully uncoiled sea serpent was zooming toward the mainland. Kumari Kandam was minutes away from an unsuspecting seaside town.

"Prepare cannons!" the admiral ordered. But just then, a loud screeching erupted from the sky. Everyone looked up.

It was Zon! Zak was on her back. They were diving straight at the sea serpent's head.

Zak held several Cortex Disrupters that had been bound together to form one large weapon. He looked like a flying high-tech knight about to joust with a dragon.

Zon screeched and dove at the sea serpent again. The huge green monster reared its head.

Once he was at eye level with the beast, Zak took a deep breath. He tried to focus his cryptidcalming powers. "Easy, you don't want to hurt us," he said soothingly.

The sea serpent paused long enough for Zak to take the Claw from his belt. The Claw amplified Zak's powers—and the leviathan was going to put them to the test.

Zak raised the Claw. He concentrated on the sea serpent. A glow appeared in Zak's eyes. The hum of mental energy grew louder and louder around him.

The sea serpent froze and its eyes glazed over for a moment. Then it let out a skull-shaking roar! It snapped at Zak and Zon, its massive jaws crashing shut.

Zon veered out of the way. Zak lost concentration and the glow faded from his eyes.

"Dang," Zak said. It had been worth a shot.

Zak reined in his nerves, raised the Cortex Disrupters, and charged!

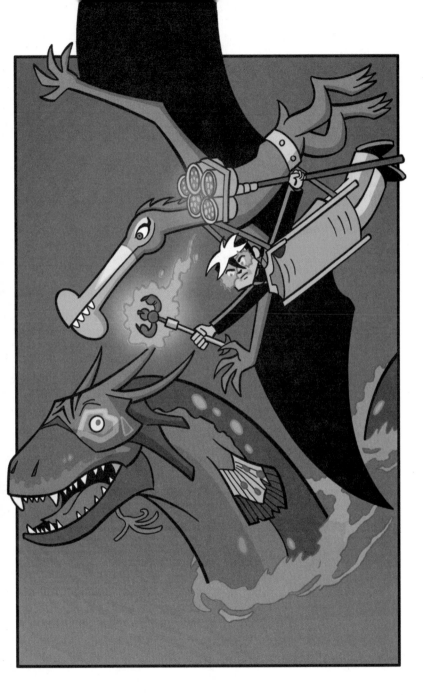

Meanwhile, Argost watched Doc and Fiskerton battle Munya. Doc grabbed one of the monster man's arms, but Munya spit a stream of web into his face. Doc thrashed and pulled at the sticky stuff, but it only stretched like rubber.

Ulraj ran to help him, but Argost raised his hand and said, "Ah, ah, ah, unfinished business, Your Highness."

Argost hadn't forgotten for a moment why he'd come to this forgotten island. It was to find the medallion.

Argost reached into the pocket of his shark-skin cape. He hurled a fistful of black seeds at Ulraj's feet.

In seconds, the seeds sprouted into long black tendrils covered with octopuslike suckers. The tendrils wrapped around Ulraj's small body, squeezing him tighter and tighter. Ulraj tried to pull the things off, but it was no use.

"Do please continue to struggle," Argost said. "The Nicaraguan Blood-Sucking Vine likes to work for its meal. Now, tell me where to find *my* medallion!"

Fiskerton saw the vines making their way to Ulraj's neck. He tried to help, but Munya hit him with a heavy stream of webbing. The force of the sticky spray pinned Fiskerton to the wall.

Munya grinned and crawled toward Fiskerton. He wanted to finish the big ape off—but suddenly Munya felt the air leave his lungs.

Doc had rammed into him from behind with the force of a freight train!

Chapter 9

Out over the Indian Ocean, Zak and Zon were dodging the giant sea serpent. The huge creature was weaving its head back and forth, trying to rid itself of Zak's and Zon's pesky presence.

Zak aimed his Cortex Disrupters, but the sea serpent wouldn't stay still.

Suddenly, a burst of cannon fire rocked the sky. Zak looked down to see Kumari cannons pointing at him!

"Another volley!" the Kumari captain ordered as his men reloaded.

Zak and Zon swerved to miss both the next blast and the snapping serpent head. It was a tough maneuver, but it gave Zak an idea.

"Zon!" he called out, pointing at the cannons. "Fly down there!"

As Zon headed toward the ground, the serpent's head followed. The Kumari soldiers saw the huge head coming at them.

"Look out!" the admiral yelled. The Kumari soldiers dove in all directions as they tried to escape the snapping green jaws.

The giant sea serpent plowed through the Kumari cannons and tossed them like small toys.

Another battle continued inside the palace as Munya turned toward Doc in a rage. His spider legs raked at Doc's face and body. Doc threw an uppercut to Munya's chin. Munya shook it off, then opened his mouth and spit another web blast.

But this time, Doc was ready. He sidestepped the stream and grabbed a strand of web in his fist. He yanked on it hard, pulling Munya's head down to meet a swift knee jab. Munya fell to the ground. He was out cold.

Doc looked over and saw that the sucker vines were trying to suffocate Ulraj. Argost was screaming, "Tell me where the medallion is!"

"Right here," Ulraj said finally, reaching into his pocket. He pulled out the medallion.

Argost smiled greedily. At last he was going to get what he'd come for.

Doc couldn't believe what he was seeing. "Ulraj!" he yelled. "I told you to leave that in the airship!"

Ulraj held the medallion up with his free arm

and spoke to it. "Medallion! Dr. Saturday tells me you hold great power! If so, show me now! As king of Kumari Kandam, I command you to strike down the man who killed my father!"

The medallion suddenly began to glow. As its light grew brighter, a low growl filled the room.

Argost looked around nervously as the red glow turned into a giant shadow. To everyone's shock, the shadow grew into a huge red-fanged beast. It let out a bloodcurdling howl and hurled itself at Argost!

Streams of red smoke flowed from the beast into Argost's nose and mouth. Argost screamed in terror.

The howl of the beast echoed far beyond the palace. Kumari soldiers everywhere covered their ears.

High in the sky, Zak hung on tightly as Zon and the sea serpent twisted wildly at the sound.

Argost dropped to his knees. He was helpless against the creature.

At the same time, the black sucker vines were still crawling up Ulraj. "Dr. Saturday!" he screamed. "I can't stop it!"

With a charging yell, Doc slammed into the vines, knocking Ulraj free. But as Ulraj fell, the medallion flew out of his hand!

It rolled over to Munya, just recovering from Doc's powerful knee jab. Munya's eyes flashed open. He grabbed the medallion, then leapt over and picked up his master.

With his long spider legs, Munya quickly climbed up a stone column.

Doc knew he had only one chance for victory. He whipped out his CP and snapped a photo of the medallion in Munya's hand.

Munya skittered out a high window with Argost and was gone.

Chapter 10

Outside the palace, the howling finally stopped. "What the heck was that?" Zak asked, taking his hands from his ears.

The Kumari soldiers shook their heads and regrouped, ready to fight again. The admiral shouted, "No more tricks from the surface men!"

He looked up at the serpent. "Ignore the boy!" he called to the monster. "Attack the city!"

The serpent turned away from Zak and slithered toward the mainland.

Beachgoers saw the green monster as its

massive head appeared over the horizon. They ran screaming in panic.

Zak wasn't about to let a war begin. "No, I won't fail you again, Mom," he said to himself.

Zak grabbed hold of the Claw. He closed his eyes, and this time, he focused as hard as he could.

His eyes glowed as the Hand of Tsul'Kula opened. Zak used every bit of his mental strength as he commanded, "Will you just! Stand! Still!"

The sea serpent suddenly became still. It seemed confused. Zak's powers worked! "I did it!" he cried.

The sea serpent started to shake off the effects of his power. "Not this time, scaly," Zak said, using a huge mental push to keep the beast calm.

Zak charged up the bundle of Cortex Disrupters and hurled them at the sea serpent's

neck. A great crackle of energy surged through the creature, knocking it unconscious.

The people on the beach cheered. Zak and Zon flew triumphantly around the giant serpent.

"Woooooo!" Zak shouted. "Did you see how big that thing was? I've got the cryptid powers *down*! Bring on Kur! Yeah! Wooooo!"

Later, inside the palace of Kumari Kandam, Ulraj took his place on the throne. He was surrounded by the Saturdays, including Drew. She had a few bandages on her arm, but she was feeling fine.

Doc activated his CP screen. He zoomed in on the digital photo of the medallion. The others looked on anxiously. Doc read the ancient Sumerian writing on the medallion: "'Before the breath of

Kur, the sentinels will fall.'"

Drew looked worried, and said, "I don't like the sound of that."

Zak nodded. His ears were still ringing from the discharge of the Cortex Disrupters. He didn't like the sound of anything at the moment. "Yeah, tell me about it," he said.

Ulraj sighed. "I am sorry, Dr. Saturday. I should have left the medallion in your airship."

"Don't worry, Your Highness," Doc told him confidently. "We'll get it back to you."

"No," Ulraj said, having learned his lesson. "I do hope you get it back, but not for me. I want you to keep it safe. I think it's been proven unwise to leave so much power in the hands of one so young and inexperienced."

Doc and Drew threw Zak a look.

Zak looked at them as if to say *What?* Then he looked down at the Cortex Disrupters in his hand. He knew exactly what his parents were thinking. He had to do something quickly.

"This is totally different," Zak said. "I disobeyed you, yes. And I'm very sorry about that. But I think I just showed that I'm responsible enough to handle a weapon like this."

Zak swung his arm up to make his point and accidentally hit the wall with the Cortex Disrupters. ZAP! The beam set a Kumari tapestry on fire.

As the flames crept up the tapestry and smoke filled the room, Zak handed the Cortex Disrupters to his mom. "Okay," he grumbled, slightly embarrassed. "You can keep it."

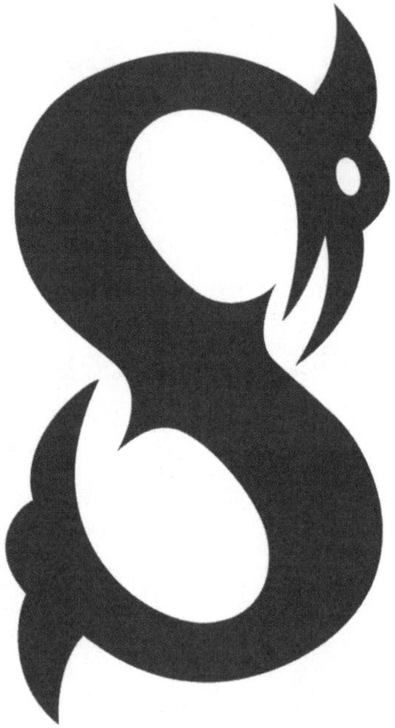